*What's the first day of the*
*Street Sharks' calendar?*

*What kind of fish interrupted the*
*sea urchins' underwater picnic?*

*What do you call a lobster that won't share?*

Give up? Read on to find the answers...

***Swim along with the chew crew as they enforce the law of the jaw!***

SHARKBAIT

LAUGH ATTACK—a Street Sharks joke book

*by Vincent Courtney*



Bullseye Books
Random House New York

A BULLSEYE BOOK PUBLISHED BY RANDOM HOUSE, INC.
 Published in the United States by Random House, Inc., New York, and simultaneously in Canada by Random House of Canada Limited, Toronto. 

Library of Congress Catalog Card Number: 95-69978
ISBN: 0-679-87708-8

Manufactured in the United States of America 10 9 8 7 6 5 4 3 2 1

## The Year of the Shark

## Chapter 1

# A Jawsome Month for Jokes!

*What's the first day of the Street Sharks' calendar?*
Jaw-nuary 1!

*Why did Dr. Piranoid hit Slobster with a bell on January 1?*
He wanted to ring in the New Year!

Ripster is one cool Street Shark.
He's their leader because he's so smart.
He's known to be clever
and relentless forever,
with courage and love in his heart!

*What do you call a friend of the Street Sharks?*
Chum!

*What are New Year's resolutions?*
Promises that go in one year and out the other!

There is a Street Shark named Streex,
who's fed up with those evil geeks.
When danger is near,
he skates without fear,
for, you see, it's trouble he seeks.

*What do sharks sing on New Year's Eve?*
"Auld Fang Syne"!

*Why did the kangaroo escape from the zoo on January 1?*
He wanted to have a hoppy New Year!

*What is the Street Sharks' favorite candy?*
Jawbreakers!

There is a Street Shark named Jab,
who eats concrete by the slab.
When he swims through the streets,
it's the concrete he eats,
because he was born in a lab!

*What do you get when you take away a lemon shark's dinner?*
A sourpuss with fins!

*Where do you park your fish?*
In a carp-port!

*How did the police inspector know who stole the fish?*
The thief looked gill-ty!

*What's the difference between a good meeting with a shark and a bad meeting with a shark?*
In the good meeting, you only lose one leg!

There is a Street Shark named Slammu,
who fights when he shouts "Slammu Jammu!"
He is a little naive,
but has strength up his sleeve.
If you work for Piranoid, he'll wham you!

*Man:* "These new alligator shoes are uncomfortable."
*Shoe salesman:* "That's because you didn't pull their teeth!"

Knock, knock!
Who's there?
Wanda.
Wanda who?
Wanda go fishing?

*What do you call a shark lawyer?*
An attorney-at-jaw!

*What kind of fish sits in a can and pouts?*
A sour-dine!

*What kind of fish sits on a throne and rules the sea?*
A king mackerel!

*What happened when Slobster ate beans every day?*
He never ran out of gas!

*What kind of fish does a skeleton put in his aquarium?*
Bonefish!

*What kind of fish does a cheerleader wave at a crowd?*
A pom-pompano!

*What kind of fish interrupted the sea urchins' underwater picnic?*
Ant-chovies!

*What kind of fish hibernates during the winter?*
A bear-acuda!

*What happened when Slash ate garlic every day?*
He was never short of breath!

*What do you get when you throw bread dough in the ocean?*
Sea biscuits!

*What kind of fish do birds like to land on?*
Speckled perches!

*What's the best kind of Italian fish soup?*
Minnow-strone!

Knock, knock!
Who's there?
Luke.
Luke who?
Luke over there, I see Dr. Piranoid!

*What do you call pants for fish?*
Trout-sers!

*What do you call a lobster that won't share?*
Shellfish!

*How did the oyster get on the roof of the house?*
He clammed up a ladder!

## Chapter 2

# Hugs and Fishes!

*Why did the duck refuse the box of candy from the Canada goose?*
Her mother always told her to beware of geese bearing gifts!

*What did the lovesick stamp say to the envelope?*
"I'm stuck on you!"

*What did the frog give his girlfriend for Valentine's Day?*
Bugs and kisses!

*Why did the man put the pickle back in the barrel?*
He thought it was no big dill!

*What did the magnet say to the refrigerator?*
"I find you very attractive!"

*SLAMMU:* "Did you hear about the time the Easter Bunny switched jobs with the Tooth Fairy?"
*JAB:* "No, what happened?"
*SLAMMU:* "All the kids woke up with eggs under their pillows!"

*Why did the shirt and the pants fall in love?*
Because they were always hanging around each other in the closet!

*What did the Street Sharks give their girlfriends for Valentine's Day?*
Hugs and fishes!

*What did the lovesick clock say to the watch?*
"Be my valen-time!"

*What did one puddle of algae say to the other?*
"Be my valen-slime!"

*What did the fireplace say to the log?*
"I love you with all my hearth!"

*What did the baker say to his wife on Valentine's Day?*
"I loaf you!"

*What did the coffee cup say to the beer mug?*
"Be my valen-stein!"

*What did one billboard say to the other billboard?*
"Be my valen-sign!"

*What did the whipped cream say to the strawberry shortcake?*
"I'm sweet on you!"

*What is the Street Sharks' favorite love song?*
"Let Me Call You Sweet-shark!"

*What did the trash compactor say to the garbage?*
"I've got a crush on you!"

*What did the potter give his wife on Valentine's Day?*
Mugs and dishes!

*What do you call two weightlifters in love?*
Sweat-hearts!

*Did you hear about the conceited Cupid?*
He shot himself with his own arrow!

*What's red and white and swims in the lake?*
A valentine carp!

*What did Streex pick up at the fish market for his girlfriend?*
A valentine cod!

*What did the accountant say to his wife on Valentine's Day?*
"How do I love thee? Let me count the ways!"

*What did the woman say to Tom Thumb?*
"Be my valen-tiny!"

*How did Cupid get away from Slobster and Slash?*
It was an arrow escape!

*Why didn't Cupid shoot an arrow into Dr. Piranoid's heart?*
Because Dr. Piranoid doesn't have one!

*What did one lovesick walrus say to the other?*
"You're my true blub!"

*What did one house say to the other?*
"Care for a little room-ance?"

*What would you get if you crossed Cupid with a hog?*
Cupig!

*What actress would Streex most like to date?*
Kim Basking Shark!

*What happened when the cotton balls met?*
It was fluff at first sight!

Knock, knock!
Who's there?
Howard.
Howard who?
Howard you like a box of chocolates?

Knock, knock!
Who's there?
Bea.
Bea who?
Bea my valentine!

*RIPSTER:* "Streex is so in love with himself, he reminds me of a virus."
*JAB:* "A virus?"
*RIPSTER:* "Yeah, he makes me sick!"

*What happened when the two lazy good-for-nothings met?*
It was slob at first sight!

*What did one doughnut say to the other?*
"I love you a hole lot!"

*Why did the lonely man envy his calendar?*
Because it had so many dates!

# Chapter 3

# Irish You'd Laugh

*SLOBSTER:* "I need to find something green for St. Patrick's Day."
*SLASH:* "Did you look up your nose?"

*What giant wooden box floats next to Ireland?*
Crate Britain!

*What Irish city has the most twins?*
Double-lin!

*What Irish instrument is made in a swamp?*
A bogpipe!

*What instrument does an Irish pest play?*
A bugpipe!

*What has fangs, a spotted green coat, and a pot o' gold?*
A leopard-chaun!

Knock, knock!
Who's there?
Irish.
Irish who?
Irish I was as cool as the Street Sharks!

*What's green, has fins, and is kissed for luck in Ireland?*
The Blarney Shark!

*What's a leprechaun's favorite dessert?*
Shortcake!

*What do you call a leprechaun gathering?*
A leprechaun-vention!

*Why don't leprechauns make good cashiers?*
Because they're always short-changing people!

*What did one Irish dancer say to the other?*
"Tap o' the morning to ya!"

*What do you call a leprechaun who carries a lantern around with him?*
A lamp-prechaun!

*What did the lovesick Irish potato say to his girlfriend?*
"I only have eyes for you!"

*What newspaper do the Street Sharks read?*
*The New Jaw-k Times*!

*What is a seabird's favorite newspaper?*
The *Gull Screech Journal*!

*How do fish smell underwater?*
Wet!

*Who is the Street Sharks' favorite musician?*
Stingray Charles!

*What's the Street Sharks' favorite soldier toy?*
G.I. Jaw!

*What kind of shark hates the color red?*
A bull shark!

*Why does Slammu cry more than his brothers?*
Because he's a wail shark!

*How does a chef chop off the heads of fish in a restaurant?*
With a gill-otine!

*To what acting union do the Street Sharks belong?*
The Screen Actors Gill!

*What's purple, swims in the sea, and loves to eat people?*
A grape white shark!

*What's the Street Sharks' favorite dessert?*
Pie à la road!

*What's the Street Sharks' favorite band?*
Stone Temple Pilotfish!

One eel tried to sue another for slippery business dealings, but he didn't have a leg to stand on!

*What's the difference between a car tire and a Street Shark?*
One the street eats, the other eats the street!

*SLASH:* "Hey, Slobster, what do you get when you cross a leprechaun and a kangaroo?"
*SLOBSTER:* "A pouch o' gold?"
*SLASH:* "No, a leap-prechaun!"

## Chapter 4

# A Basketful of Sharkles

*What do chickens celebrate on April 1?*
April Fowl's Day!

*SLASH:* "Hey, Slobster, how many comedians does it take to pull a practical joke?"
*SLOBSTER:* "I don't know. How heavy is the joke?"

*What do you get when you cross a hen and a comedian?*
Eggs full of jokes instead of yolks!

*What do monsters celebrate on April 1?*
April Ghoul's Day!

*Did you hear about the farmer who bought two million gallons of pig soap?*
That sounds like a lot of hogwash to me!

*Why didn't Slammu eat his chocolate bunnies?*
He was waiting for them to multiply!

*Where did the Easter Bunny go to college?*
University of Hare-izona!

*Why couldn't Jab prove that Slammu ate some of his chocolate eggs?*
Because he didn't know the eggsact number in his basket!

*What happened when the Easter Bunny tripped on Streex's skates?*
He scrambled the colored eggs!

*Who delivers Easter baskets to all the fish in the ocean?*
The Oyster Bunny!

*How do you catch the Easter Bunny?*
Dig a hole in the ground and act like a carrot!

*Did you hear the one about the Easter Bunny who sat on a tack?*
It was a hare-raising tale!

*What is the Easter Bunny's motto?*
Hare today, gone tomorrow!

*Why didn't Ripster believe that Slammu ate a ten-foot-tall chocolate bunny?*
It was a little hard to swallow!

*Why did the tooth fairy hide Easter eggs under the kid's pillow?*
Because she didn't have any cents!

*How did the Easter Bunny feel when he lost his favorite basket?*
He was hopping mad!

*What would you get if you crossed the Easter Bunny with Slobster?*
The Easter Bonehead!

*When is the best time to look for Easter eggs?*
On Easter, of course!

*What happened when Dr. Piranoid traded places with the Easter Bunny?*
On Easter, all the kids got rotten eggs!

*What is Dr. Piranoid's favorite Easter treat?*
Jelly-genes!

*Why did the bald farmer stop raising rabbits?*
He lost all his hairs!

*Where did the Easter Bunny hide the eggs at Dr. Piranoid's laboratory?*
In the gene pool!

*Why did Slobster run the lawn mower over his Easter basket?*
He thought the plastic grass was too high!

*How does the Easter Bunny deliver all those eggs in one day?*
He uses Federal Eggspress!

*What happened when the Easter Bunny let his friend, the duck, deliver some of his eggs?*
The duck quacked them!

*SLASH:* "Slobster, Dr. Piranoid's gonna kill you when he sees that messy pan."
*SLOBSTER:* "How was I supposed to know that you can't fry chocolate eggs?"

*What happened to the chocolate bunny who escaped from the Easter basket?*
He lived hoppily ever after!

*What do you get when you cross a clown with a certain kind of Easter candy?*
Jolly-beans!

*What do you get when you cross a purple vegetable with a particular type of Easter treat?*
Jelly-beets!

*What has sharp teeth, carries a basket, and goes hippity chomp, hippity chomp, hippity chomp?*
The Easter Shark!

*Why was the Easter Bunny angry?*
He was having a bad hare day!

*What kind of Easter candy is made from dead fish?*
Smelly-beans!

*What is the Street Sharks' favorite Easter treat?*
What *isn't* the Street Sharks' favorite Easter treat?

*SLAMMU:* "Hey, Streex, how did you get that black eye?"
*STREEX:* "From eating jellybeans."
*SLAMMU:* "Jellybeans? You can't get a black eye from eating jellybeans."
*STREEX:* "You can if they belong to Jab!"

## Chapter 5

# Mother, May I Giggle?

*What did the Street Sharks get their mother for Mother's Day?*
A lunch of flowers!

*What did the baker get his mother on Mother's Day?*
A bouquet of flours!

*How did the mother gorilla like her Mother's Day gift?*
She went bananas!

*How did the mother sheep like her Mother's Day gift?*
She thought it wasn't baaah-d!

*What did the mute call his mother?*
"Mum" is the word!

*DR. PIRANOID'S MOTHER:* "Why did you get me dead flowers for Mother's Day?"
*DR. PIRANOID:* "Because I couldn't find any rotten candy!"

*What did they call the first woman who tried to fly without a parachute?*
The martyr of invention!

Knock, knock!
Who's there?
Mommy.
Mommy who?
Mommy and my brothers want to wish you a happy Mother's Day!

*What did the considerate fisherman give his mother for Mother's Day?*
A Mother's Day cod!

*What did the noisy fisherman give his mother for Mother's Day?*
A headache!

*What did the mother strawberry say to the baby strawberry?*
"Don't get caught in a jam!"

*SLASH:* "Hey Slobster, you know why your mother doesn't call you her son?"
*SLOBSTER:* "I dunno, why?"
*SLASH:* "Because you're not too bright!"

*What did the prizefighter give his mother for Mother's Day?*
A boxer of chocolates!

*Snake:* "Hey, Mom, we're going out for Mother's Day dinner."
*Mother snake:* "Where are we going?"
*Snake:* "Someplace where they don't charge an arm and a leg!"

*How did the mother elf feel after her son gave her a bouquet of flowers?*
She was fairy happy!

*What happened when Slammu dropped his mother's birthday cake with its candles lit?*
It was de-lighted!

*What did the firefighter get his mother for Mother's Day?*
Panty-hose!

*How did the mother bee react when she got a flower arrangement for Mother's Day?*
She was all abuzz!

*What holiday in May do Slobster and Slash celebrate?*
Mugger's Day!

*What holiday in May do Egyptians celebrate?*
Mummy's Day!

*What famous mother invented the telescope?*
Old Mother Hubble!

*What saintly famous mother was also the first lady lumberjack?*
Mother Tree-saw!

*SLAMMU:* "Hey, Jab, I made Mom an upside-down cake for Mother's Day."
*JAB:* "But I thought you were making a chocolate cake."
*SLAMMU:* "I was, but I dropped it!"

*What was the sailor after his round-the-world trip with his mother?*
A mama's buoy!

*What did the female shark say to her mother?*
"I never met a man I didn't bite!"

*What famous mother worked at a Las Vegas chapel?*
Mother Marry!

*What do you call a mom who's a gangster?*
A mother hood!

*Why did the Street Sharks commission a sculptor to make a statue of their mom?*
They wanted a mother figure!

*What do you call a mom who's an attorney?*
A mother-in-law!

*What famous mom controls the weather?*
Mother Nature!

Knock, knock!
Who's there?
Wendy.
Wendy who?
Wendy-livering flowers on Mother's Day, always make sure you're at the right address!

# Chapter 6

# Who Invited the Wedding Jests?

*What did the tailor do after he fell in love with a pair of trousers?*
He wed his pants!

*What did the baker say to his bride on their wedding day?*
"I dough!"

*What did the chef say to his bride on his wedding day?*
"I stew!"

*"Why do you wear your wedding ring on your thumb?"*
"Because my husband and I met hitchhiking!"

*Where do fish get married?*
At the wetting chapel!

*STREEX:* "Did you read in the paper where Hedda Jones married Bob Lettus?"
*JAB:* "Yeah, now she's Hedda Lettus!"

*What do you call a woman who marries a hungry shark?*
A honeymoon sweet!

*What do you call a bale of hay that marries a hungry horse?*
The fodder of the bride!

*What happened to the two maple trees that got married?*
They lived sappily ever after!

There was a man who promised his wife a chicken farm.
So he bought her a dozen eggs and told her to wait!

*Why did the traveling salesman marry the elephant?*
So he'd never forget his trunk!

A man married his doctor, but found out later that she didn't have any patients!

*Why didn't the zombie ever get married?*
He couldn't find the right ghoul!

*STREEX:* "Did you read where Bea Nancy Taylor married Bill Sillee?"
*JAB:* "Now she's Bea N. Sillee!"

*Why didn't the skeleton ever get married?*
He didn't have any guts!

*STREEX:* "Did you read where Marsha Jillian married Albert Mellow?"
*JAB:* "Now she's Marsha Mellow!"

*Woman:* "How do you find your husband now that you're married?"
*Other woman:* "Usually on the sofa, watching television!"

A tree branch married a root, but divorced it because it wouldn't grow up!

*STREEX:* "Did you read where Bea N. Sillee got a divorce and married Bob Foowelesh?"
*JAB:* "Now she's Bea N. Foowelesh!"

*What does a bead of water say when it gets married?*
"I dew!"

*What does a rooster say when it gets married?*
"I cock-a-doodle do!"

*What does a surfer say when he gets married?*
"I dude!"

*SLOBSTER:* "Hey, Slash, I heard your dog got married. How does he like it?"
*SLASH:* "He can't complain."
*SLOBSTER:* "That's good."
*SLASH:* "No, it's not. He can't complain because his wife makes him wear a muzzle!"

There was a man who promised his wife the moon. So he put her in a rocket and launched her into space!

*What do cows do after they get married?*
They go on their honeymoo!

*What's a pickle's favorite honeymoon spot?*
Going over Niagara Falls in a barrel!

*Why did the preacher let the doughnuts get married in his church?*
Because they were already holey!

*"Why do you take off your wedding ring every time you clean your hands?"*
"Because I don't want my marriage to be washed up!"

## Chapter 7

# Fireworks, Picnics, and Pranks

*What shark signed the Declaration of Independence?*
Jaw-n Hancock!

*SLAMMU:* "How did you like the fireworks?"
*RIPSTER:* "They were spark-tacular!"

*What do ghosts roast at their Fourth of July picnic?*
Hallowieners!

*What do you put in cold oyster stew to warm it up?*
Firecrackers!

*What do you get when you put swim fins on a mule?*
Kicked!

*Why didn't the vampire ever go to the beach?*
He didn't want to make an ash out of himself!

*What's the difference between a lawn-care service and a baby-sitting service?*
One mows lawns, the other loans moms!

*How can you tell if a dog has been running?*
Look at his pants!

*What do you call a fish that eats all the beans at the family picnic?*
A stinkray!

*What's the difference between a picnic basket and the Street Sharks' stomachs?*
You can fill up a picnic basket!

*SLASH:* "Hey, Slobster, did you know that monsters have their own Constitution?"
*SLOBSTER:* "They do?"
*SLASH:* "Yes—haven't you ever heard of the Bill of Frights?"

*"Hey, Dr. Piranoid, why do you have a pickle behind your ear?"*
"Oh, no, I must have eaten my pencil!"

*Where's the best place to find fried fish?*
Between two slices of bread!

*Why was the sushi chef shocked when he sliced the fish?*
Because it was an electric eel!

*SLASH:* "Hey, Slobster, what kind of fish eats poisoned bait?"
*SLOBSTER:* "The stupid kind!"

Knock, knock!
Who's there?
Alec.
Alec who?
Alec your face if you get too close!

Knock, knock!
Who's there?
Dr. Piranoid, the mad scientist.
See ya!

Knock, knock!
Who's there?
Hedda.
Hedda who?
Hedda hot dog for you, but Slammu ate it!

Knock, knock!
Who's there?
Candy.
Candy who?
Candy Street Sharks defeat de evil Dr. Piranoid?

*What do you call a fisherman with binoculars?*
Seymour!

The animal rights people arrested the chef because he was battering his fish!

*What should you do if you see a great big old shark?*
Hope it doesn't see little old you!

*Captain Ahab:* "I heard Moby Dick surface next to the *Pequod* last night, so I got up and caught him in my pajamas!"
*First mate:* "What was Moby Dick doing in your pajamas?"

*What did Jab and Streex do at the family picnic?*
Pitched horseshoe crabs!

*SLOBSTER:* "Dr. Piranoid, I just invented something that can look through walls."
*DR. PIRANOID:* "You idiot, that's a window!"

*Why did the farmer give his chickens paint instead of water to drink?*
He wanted them to lay colored eggs!

*What do you call a baby catfish?*
A kittenfish!

*How many of Dr. Piranoid's mutants does it take to change a light bulb?*
Two—one to bite off the old bulb and one to hammer in the new bulb!

*What did the man see after he was run over by a herd of zebras?*
Stars and stripes forever!

*What do you call a three-thousand-pound great white shark?*
Anything it wants!

*Why wasn't the woman afraid of sharks?*
Because they're man-eaters!

# Chapter 8

# Summer Snickers!

*What did the ice fisherman catch without using any bait?*
A cold!

*What do you call a baby bear that makes a hole in one?*
A golf cub!

Knock, knock!
Who's there?
Jab.
Jab who?
Jab-a dabba doo!

*What do you get when you cross an octopus with a slot machine?*
An eight-armed bandit!

*What do you get when you pull Dr. Piranoid's teeth?*
Chewing gums!

Knock, knock!
Who's there?
Norma Lee.
Norma Lee who?
Norma Lee I ring the doorbell!

Knock, knock!
Who's there?
Bear.
Bear who?
Bear open the door before I knock it down!

*What's huge, has giant fangs, and terrorizes the refrigerator?*
Slammu!

*What do you call a shark circling a sinking lifeboat?*
Lucky!

*Why did the safecracker put TNT in his handkerchief?*
He needed to blow his nose!

*SLASH:* "Hey, Slobster, what do get when you cross a cow with a clown?"
*SLOBSTER:* "Someone who's udderly ridiculous!"

*How does a Street Shark know when it's time to eat?*
He's awake!

Knock, knock!
Who's there?
Slam.
Slam who?
Slammu is one of the Street Sharks!

*What do you get when you cross a ten-year-old buggy driver and a deep-sea fish?*
A young whipper-snapper!

Knock, knock!
Who's there?
Bluefish.
Bluefish who?
Bluefish out of the water with dynamite!

*Where do fish sleep?*
In riverbeds!

*How does a Street Shark floss his razor-sharp teeth?*
Very carefully!

"I just saw a Street Shark with a mouthful of fangs."
*"I don't believe you."*
"Well, it's the tooth!"

Knock, knock!
Who's there?
You.
You who?
You who, it's me!

*Why did Jab take a dose of aspirin?*
He had a haddock!

*Did you hear about the chivalrous Street Shark?*
He was a bite in shining armor!

*What's the best kind of bait to catch a seahorse?*
Sea oats!

*What do deaf fish use to hear better?*
Herring aids!

*What do you call a shark packed in a box of snow?*
A crated white shark!

*What kind of shark can you find in a toolbox?*
A hammerhead!

*SLOBSTER:* "Hey, Slash, I'm going to go to the masquerade party as something big, ugly, and mean."
*SLASH:* "What? I thought you were wearing a costume!"

*What does Slobster eat on his birthday?*
Crabcake!

*Customer:* "Waiter, do you have crab legs?"
*Waiter:* "Yes."
*Customer:* "Well, don't worry about it, my cousin's pigeon-toed!"

*DR. PIRANOID:* "Now I want you to go to the window, cross your eyes, and stick out your tongue."
*SLASH:* "Will that cure my cold?"
*DR. PIRANOID:* "No. I just don't like my neighbor!"

*What happened when the chicken broke the mirror?*
He got seven years' bad cluck!

*What do you call a thirsty Street Shark?*
A fish out of water!

Knock, knock!
Who's there?
Ladyfish.
Ladyfish who?
Ladyfish over here, and you might catch something!

## Chapter 9

# A School of Fish Jokes

*What is the Street Sharks' favorite class?*
Al-jaw-bra!

*SLASH:* "Hey, Slobster, did you hear about the cafeteria worker who got fired after she put the condiments in the freezer?"
*SLOBSTER:* "No. Why'd she get fired for that?"
*SLASH:* "Because she couldn't cut the mustard!"

The geometry teacher tried to punish Slobster by making him stand in the corner, but the dummy couldn't find it!

*What is Slammu's favorite class?*
Gastronomy!

*What do you get when you cross a basketball coach and a flower?*
A gym dandelion!

*Why didn't the snake take football class?*
He knew he couldn't pass!

The chemistry professor couldn't teach the unruly kids because they kept throwing things atom!

*What kind of horse attends shop class?*
A sawhorse!

*What is the Street Sharks' favorite country?*
Finland!

*Where do sharks learn?*
In schools!

*What country is most like the Street Sharks?*
Hungary!

Knock, knock!
Who's there?
Tony.
Tony who?
Tony, ankle, foot—these are the parts of my leg!

Knock, knock!
Who's there?
Catfish.
Catfish who?
Catfish with claws, dogfish with paws!

*Teacher:* "If you had to divide one fish among eight sharks, what would you get?"
*Student:* "Eight hungry sharks!"

*Man:* "If you had to choose between hearing and smelling, which would you choose?"
*Other man:* "I'd pick my nose!"

*Who was the first shark to swim the Atlantic Ocean?*
Charles Finbergh!

*Which president liked to eat three-day-old fish?*
Abraham Stinkin'!

*How does Slammu count?*
"One, tooth, three..."

*SLASH:* "Hey, Slobster, how many fish does it take to make a school?"
*SLOBSTER:* "That depends on the size. Is it an elementary school or a college?"

*SLASH:* "Hey, Slobster, have you got a dollar for a tuna sandwich?"
*SLOBSTER:* "I don't know. Let me see the sandwich!"

*SLASH:* "Hey, Slobster, what does your watch say?"
*SLOBSTER:* "It doesn't say anything. You have to look at it!"

*What do you call a fish that drives a BMW?*
A yuppie guppy!

*What kind of shark likes to swim by itself?*
A lone shark!

*SLOBSTER:* "What do you call a group of seahorses?"
*SLASH:* "A herd of them."
*SLOBSTER:* "I know you heard of them. But what are they called!"

*What kind of fish ride on airplanes?*
Flying fish!

*What's the Street Sharks' favorite Mark Twain novel?*
*Huckleberry Fin!*

*What kind of fish ride in buses?*
Bassengers!

*Why did Streex take all his money and convert it into pennies?*
Because he wanted some change in his life!

*Who was the first president to come out of a can?*
George Washingtuna!

*What bird lives under the ocean?*
A sea robin!

*What kind of shark has wings and a halo?*
An angel shark!

*What do you call a fish that rock-and-rolls?*
A jammin' salmon!

*Who was the first caveman to catch a shark?*
Fred Fishstone!

*SLASH:* "Hey, Slobster, I once knew a whaling captain with one leg named Ahab."
*SLOBSTER:* "Oh, yeah? What was the name of his other leg?"

# Chapter 10

## Fintastically Funny Frights!

*What do you get when you cross Slobster with a pumpkin?*
A jerk-o'-lantern!

*Vampire to female zombie:* What's a nice ghoul like you doing in a place like this?

*What breakfast food haunts the kitchen?*
Casper the friendly toast!

*What did the ghost put in his coffee?*
Non-dairy screamer!

*What do fishermen say on Halloween?*
"Trick or trout!"

*Why didn't the Street Sharks cross the scary-looking bridge?*
Because they couldn't pay the troll!

There is a ghoul named Fred,
who loves to eat parts of the dead.
He starts with the toes,
and then upward he goes,
finishing up with the head!

*Who has sharp teeth, fins, and bolts in his neck?*
Frankenshark!

*Why did Dracula file his fangs?*
He wanted to make a point!

*What kind of monster operates a moving truck?*
A vanpire!

*What is a vampire's least favorite food?*
A cold steak!

*What is a vampire's favorite drink?*
A Bloody Mary!

*Why didn't Jab like vampires?*
He thought they were a pain in the neck!

*Why didn't Slammu like the mummy?*
He thought he was too wrapped up in himself!

*Why didn't Ripster like jack-o'-lanterns?*
He thought they were airheads!

*What happened when the ghoul met the goblin?*
They became the best of fiends!

*What do lumberjacks say on Halloween?*
"Trick or tree!"

*What's the tallest building in Transylvania?*
The Vampire State Building!

*What did the witch say to her long-lost sister?*
"You're a fright for sore eyes!"

*What did the boy ghost say to his girlfriend?*
"I think you're boo-tiful!"

*SLASH:* "Hey, Slobster, what does a werewolf call his dinner date?"
*SLOBSTER:* "Dessert!"

*Why did the mad scientist stop making the monster?*
Because he didn't have the heart to keep going!

*Why did all the spirits listen to the ghost of the poet?*
Because he was so well spooken!

*How far did the haunted plane fly on Halloween?*
From ghost to ghost!

*What spirit haunted the television talk show?*
The Phantom of the Oprah!

*What do the Street Sharks like to drink on Halloween?*
Ghoul-Aid!

*Did you hear about the ghost that lived by the pond?*
He liked to haunt ducks!

*What game do little ghosts like to play?*
Hide-and-shriek!

*SLASH:* "Hey, Slobster, you sure are ugly and scary tonight."
*DR. PIRANOID:* "Just wait until he puts on his Halloween mask!"

*Why didn't the Street Sharks see the ghost on Halloween night?*
They were too busy goblin down their candy!

# Chapter 11

# Let's Shark Turkey!

*SLASH:* "Hey, Slobster, why are you stuffing all that turkey in your mouth?"

*SLOBSTER:* "It tastes better than stuffing it in my nose!"

*How did you know if the early New England settlers were happy?*
By their pil-grins!

*Why did Slammu blush when he went into the kitchen on Thanksgiving?*
He saw the turkey dressing!

*What do you get when you invite the Street Sharks over for Thanksgiving dinner?*
No leftovers!

*What's black and white and red all over?*
An embarrassed Pilgrim!

*How did the fish in the aquarium celebrate Thanksgiving?*
They were very tankful!

*How did the genius celebrate Thanksgiving?*
He was very thinkful!

*How did the court jester celebrate Thanksgiving?*
He was very thankfool!

*Why didn't the Street Sharks go for seconds on Thanksgiving?*
Because they ate everything the first time!

*What did the Street Sharks say to the Thanksgiving turkey?*
"Pleased to eat you!"

*What is a monarch's favorite Thanksgiving dessert?*
Pumpking pie!

*What is a mathematician's favorite Thanksgiving dessert?*
Pumpkin pi!

*What kind of dessert do you make out of sand?*
Beach cobbler!

*What do you get if you cross a turkey and a Georgia fruit?*
A peach gobbler!

*What November holiday do hot dogs celebrate?*
Franksgiving!

*Why did Streex pour black ink all over Jab's turkey?*
Because he said he liked dark meat!

*What kind of fish makes the best soup?*
The kind that went to cooking school!

*How do you get milk from a horse?*
Send him to the grocery store!

*SLASH:* "When was the last time you had a home-cooked meal?"
*SLOBSTER:* "Never. My home can't cook!"

*What is Dr. Piranoid's favorite Thanksgiving meal?*
Street Sharks' fin soup!

*What do the Street Sharks like to eat for dessert?*
Jell-O-fish!

*What's the difference between a great white shark and the host at a restaurant?*
One loves to eat, the other loves to greet!

*Why did the shark stop eating the tacky tourist?*
Because he didn't have any taste!

*What's the difference between a fisherman and a deli owner?*
One catches fish, the other fetches knish!

*What did the Pilgrims use to make their bread?*
Mayflour!

*How does Slammu like his mashed potatoes and gravy?*
In his stomach!

*What is the Street Sharks' favorite place to see a turkey?*
On the dining-room table!

*What did the turkey say when he met the butcher just before Thanksgiving?*
"Quack! Quack!"

*What is Slobster's favorite part of the turkey?*
The dumbstick!

*Why didn't the Street Sharks make a lettuce salad for Thanksgiving?*
They couldn't get ahead!

*What did the Street Sharks say about their turkey dinner?*
"It was fintastic!"

*What did Dr. Piranoid get when he mixed the genes of a turkey and a great white shark?*
A gobbler that gobbled up everything in sight!

*Did you hear about the gobbler that was always causing trouble in the barnyard?*
He was a jerky turkey!

*"Did you hear about the man who tried to eat a whole whale in one sitting?"*
"No, what happened?"
*"He blubbered for an hour and then quit!"*

## Chapter 12

# Santa Jaws Is Clowning to Town

*Who delivers Christmas presents to crustaceans?*
Santa Claws!

*What is the Street Sharks' favorite holiday song?*
"I'm Dreaming of a Bite Christmas!"

*Who brings the Street Sharks gifts?*
Santa Jaws!

*What does Dr. Piranoid use to tie his Christmas presents?*
A ribbonfish!

*What's the difference between Santa Claus and the Tooth Fairy?*
Santa Claus can't fit a bicycle under your pillow!

*Why did Ripster want a billiard table for Christmas?*
Because he's a real pool shark!

*What else did Ripster want for Christmas?*
A pair of cowboy bites!

*Who is Ripster's favorite detective?*
Sherlockjaw Holmes!

*What did Ripster say to Streex on the first day of December?*
"Only 24 chomping days till Christmas!"

*What kind of fish did the rich boxer have at his Christmas party?*
Smacked salmon!

*Why did the opera singer have such a hard time putting paper and ribbons on her Christmas presents?*
Because she didn't know how to rap!

*What's the difference between Frosty the Snowman and Slobster?*
One has snow brains, the other has no brains!

*Why did Jab get into trouble when he ate the model train set?*
He bit off more than he could choo-choo!

*What's the best thing you can get Streex for Christmas?*
A mirror!

*What is the Street Sharks' favorite Christmas carol?*
"Silent Bite"!

*What did Dr. Piranoid want for Christmas?*
A new pair of genes!

*Why did Santa replace his elves with elephants?*
Because they work for peanuts!

*Why did the children want to get Santa's elves' autographs?*
They're so well gnome!

*Why is Jab like an angry elf?*
They both have short tempers!

*What do you get when you throw Santa's little helpers into a pile of mud?*
Brownies!

*What did the shark want for Christmas?*
A bite-cycle!

*Who's red and white and needs to be ironed?*
Kriss Crinkled!

*Who wears thick glasses, a pocket protector, and wrote* A Christmas Carol?
Charles Dorkens!

*What happened when Santa stepped on the cat's tail?*
Santa Clawed!

*Who brings presents and wrote the medical book* How Blood Coagulates?
Santa Clots!

*SLOBSTER:* "Hey, Slash, who was the most well informed of Santa's reindeer?"
*SLASH:* "Rudolph the read-news reindeer!"

*Which reindeer moonlights on Valentine's Day?*
Cupid!

*Who goes "Ho-ho-ho-owwwww"?*
Santa going down a lit chimney!

*What does a Street Shark toy have on its back?*
Doll fins!

*What do you call the last joke in a joke book?*
The end!